West 7th Street Series

THE
GUMMA
WARS

David Haynes

SUMMIT
BOOKS

Perfection Learning®

Illustrator: Laura J. Bryant

For information, contact
Perfection Learning® Corporation
1000 North Second Avenue, P.O. Box 500
Logan, Iowa 51546-0500.
Phone: 800-831-4190 • Fax: 712-644-2392

Paperback ISBN 0-7891-5414-5
Cover Craft® ISBN 0-7569-0072-7
Printed in the U.S.A.

Table of Contents

Too Many Gummas

TONY R'S BIRTHDAY party is the best thing that could happen to a guy. Ever since we started the West 7th Wildcats in Mrs. Harper's third-grade class, the Wildcats have looked forward to Tony R's birthday the same way guys look forward to Christmas and Halloween. So what if Tony R gets all the presents.

We had been planning Tony R's birthday party since summer vacation began. Not that there was much to plan. The party was mostly the same every year. All the guys go to Tony R's house right after baseball practice on the Saturday before his birthday. (His birthday isn't really until the next week, but we always have the party on Saturday, no matter what.)

We take our sleeping bags. Tony R's ma makes tacos and nachos and things like that. (The Rodriguezes are Mexican Americans.) After we eat a lot of tacos, we play Nintendo 64. (I am the best at all the Mario games.) Later Tony R's aunts and uncles come over. They sing a song for him in Spanish, and we have the cake and ice cream. Then Tony R opens his presents. After that it's scary movies and wrestling all night long.

Tony R has great parents! They know that guys like to make a little noise and have a pillow fight or two. They don't go ballistic like some parents. Like mine, for instance.

"You boys try not to break anything," Mr. Rodriguez always says to us at the party.

We say we will try not to. Mr. and Mrs. Rodriguez are smart. The day of the party they move all the breakable junk out of the basement.

The next morning we get up for cartoons and doughnuts. If we behave, and if we clean up the basement, and if we don't tease Tony R's little sisters too much, then Mr. Rodriguez will take all us Wildcats to Show Biz for pizza and then to the Mall of America.

Imagine—a party that lasts a whole day and a whole night.

This year Tony R turns 12. The oldest Wildcat of us all! The party should be slamming.

My name is Lawrence Jackson Underwood, but

the boys all call me Lu. That's what my initials spell when you take out the Jackson part. I'm 11, and I'm also a West 7th Wildcat—since third grade, like most of the others. The Wildcats are a bunch of us guys who live near West 7th Street in St. Paul. That's why we call ourselves the West 7th Wildcats.

Some people think we're a gang. They think so because when they see the Wildcats, they see two black kids—me and Bobby Samson—and two Hmong boys—Tou Vue and Johnny Vang. Johnny Vang's real name is some word I can't pronounce, but he calls himself Johnny Vang. You have to say both *Johnny* and *Vang* or he won't answer you. He says *Johnny* is a cool American name.

The other two Wildcats are Tony R, who, like I said, is Mexican American, and Kevin, who is just a regular white kid with blond hair and everything. People always ask Kevin why he wants to hang around with a gang.

"It's not a gang. It's a club," Kevin says. He is as cool as he wants to be.

I had saved up $12 and some change toward Tony R's birthday. Tou Vue and I were going to go in on a Super Soaker for a present, and we hoped to have some money left over for some other junk too. This was going to be the best party ever!

On the Wednesday before Tony R's party, I had just come home from baseball practice. Moms was on the phone.

"Yes, Mother," she said. "I'm aware of that. Yes."

"Hi, Moms," I said as I passed her on my way to my room. She rolled her eyes at me and continued winding herself up in the phone cord. She looked like a mummy wrapped up in that wire.

"Mother, we've already talked about this. You're going to have to call Denise yourself . . . Mother!"

While I was in my room counting my money to make sure I had enough, Moms came in.

"Larry," she said. Moms calls me *Larry*. She says if she wanted to call me *Lu*, she would have put that on my birth certificate in the first place. "Larry, I hope you haven't forgotten what Saturday is."

Forgotten! Tony R's birthday party should be a national holiday.

"I'm seeing how much I've got for a present right now," I told her.

"What a good grandson. That was Gumma Jackson on the phone. She's got a big day planned for the two of you on Saturday." Moms went back to the kitchen.

Eek! This year Gumma Jackson's birthday fell on the Saturday of Tony R's party! How could I have forgotten? Tony R's birthday was on the 18th of June, and Gumma Jackson's was June 15.

I scooped my money into my secret hiding place— an Air Jordans shoe box, which I had disguised to look like a science project gone bad. Before I could put on my best sweet-talking smile, Moms met me at the door of my bedroom.

"Another thing is going to happen Saturday," she said. "And it might cause a little problem. You're a big boy, and I know you can handle it."

Good old Moms. I might not have to do as much sweet talking as I thought.

"Your Aunt Denise down in Milwaukee is coming home from the hospital with her new baby tomorrow," said Moms. "I promised I'd help them get settled. Your father and I are driving down there on Friday, and we'll be spending the weekend."

Yeah! Tony R's party and the house all to myself. Party!

"Gumma Underwood is staying here with you," Moms said.

"What? Moms! I'm almost 12. I can stay by myself," I argued.

"Well, maybe in a couple of years you can, but your father has already arranged this. He's bringing Gumma over tomorrow afternoon."

"But what about Tony R's party?" I whined. Moms doesn't like whining, but I couldn't help myself. This could ruin everything.

Moms tousled my hair. "You're still going to the party. I talked with Antonio's mother and told her you'd be there before supper."

"Good," I said. I gave her a high five.

"After you're all done celebrating with Gumma Jackson," she added. It was her turn to put on her sweet-talking smile.

9

"Moms! Gumma Jackson and Gumma Underwood on the same weekend?" I whined once again.

"That's the little problem I was talking about," Moms said, almost apologetically.

Gumma Jackson and Gumma Underwood can't stand each other. Why? So many reasons I can never remember them all. The Jacksons live in St. Paul and the Underwoods are in Minneapolis. Gumma Jackson goes to the Baptist church and Gumma Underwood is a Democrat. One likes roses and one likes lilies; one pistachio ice cream, the other strawberry. It goes on and on and on. Having them together is like oil and water. They do not mix.

It used to be that on the holidays we would go from one house to the other and eat two different turkey dinners, and both gummas would fight over who got to keep us longer. Everybody's feelings got hurt.

"Enough is enough," Pops had said at last. Now we have holidays here at our house. Both gummas come. They make faces at each other while Pops slices the turkey.

I had to stop this before it was too late.

"Can't you tell Gumma Jackson something came up? We can celebrate her birthday next weekend," I said.

"Larry, you are her only grandchild," Moms said. "She would be so disappointed, and I'd never hear the end of it."

"I'm not either her only grandchild. There's Aunt Denise's new baby. Hey! There's an idea. Why don't you and Pops take Gumma Jackson with you to see the new kid?" I asked.

"Me in the car with *that* woman for seven hours? Boy, you must have lost your mind. I'm going to vacuum before that *other* woman gets here to start in on me." Moms shuffled out the door as if her feet were made out of bricks. She stuck her head back in, smiled, and said, "Y'all have fun, you hear?"

Right then I knew this was going to be the worst weekend of my life.

Shopping Spree #1

THE WEST 7TH Wildcats have a clubhouse. Well, really, it's just a garden shed—the kind that people put their lawn mowers and fertilizer in. Last summer Bobby's mom built a new garage, and now she keeps all of her gardening equipment in there. So the shed is empty and just sitting there until Bobby's mom figures out what to do with it. In the meantime it's our clubhouse, and we hope she takes a long time to figure out another use for it.

On Thursday, Tou Vue and I were sitting in the clubhouse waiting for Bobby and his mom. Ms. Samson was going to take us shopping.

Bobby's mom is the strictest mom of all. At least if you listen to Bobby she is. She never lets him do anything fun until after all his homework and chores are done and his room is picked up and everything is what she calls "shipshape."

Bobby lives with his mom and his three-year-old brother, Donald—whom we call Alf. We call him Alf because he drags with him everywhere an ugly old stuffed toy called Alf that someone gave him. As far as we can figure, Alf must have been a TV show from the olden days, and it must have been about ugly dolls or something.

"Don't call my precious boy *Alf*," Bobby's mom says, but she laughs when she says it. She may be strict, but she is pretty nice. She always has cookies around and lets us wait in the clubhouse until Bobby finishes his work.

"How much does a Super Soaker cost?" Tou Vue asked me.

"I think . . ." I said and squinted my eyes. I tried to look like I was trying hard to remember, but I really didn't know the price. I always forget to look at prices unless I really want something for myself and Moms and Pops are making me buy it with my own money.

"I think I don't know," I said. "But I think I remember that one time they were on sale, and maybe we could get it for . . . $15. I think."

"Fifteen dollars! That's a lot." Tou Vue sat on a milk crate and put his feet up on another one. His back was against the wall of the clubhouse, and soon he looked worried.

"We can always buy something cheaper," I said.

"Yeah, we could," said Tou Vue. "But that might look kinda bad. He's having a big party for us. He always gets us good presents."

Tou Vue, like I said, is Hmong. He was born in St. Paul, but his family came from over in Asia someplace. By Vietnam, he told us, but when I went to look on the map, I couldn't find a country called *Hmong*. Tou Vue said that's because when his parents

13

lived over there, his people didn't really have their own country. They lived in a place called *Laos* and in other countries too.

Tony R said that place sounded "lousy," trying to make a joke about it. But Tou Vue didn't laugh.

Tou Vue says his parents want to go back to Asia sometimes, but that he is an American now—and he is too. He likes the same kinds of food and watches the same shows and is no different from any other American kid. Sometimes he and Johnny Vang say things to each other in another language. It's usually when they are mad at each other or when we are playing capture the flag over at River Road School and they want to say something in code. And sometimes their English isn't perfect—they leave a word out or have trouble saying it right. But so what? These guys are everything you'd want in a friend, and the Wildcats wouldn't be the same without them.

I asked Tou Vue how much money he had.

"Six dollars," he said. "But maybe I can get a little more."

"I saved 12," I told him. "That *should* be enough."

When Bobby and his mom finished the laundry, Bobby's mom was ready to take us to the discount store to buy our birthday gifts.

Bobby's mom doesn't believe in toy guns, so she told Bobby to get something educational—like one of those strategy games or something. Johnny Vang has

a cousin who works at the music store, so he had
already gotten a bunch of good CDs for the party. We
didn't know what Kevin would bring.

"It's a surprise, guys," he had told us, putting on a
big suspicious grin. Kevin is a cutup. He always ends
up sitting in the hall at school for making rude noises
or passing around disrespectful drawings of the
teacher. His gifts are always crazy and always the hit
of the party. Last year he took a whole bunch of Silly
String to Tony R's party, and we had the best
wrestling match ever—everybody was all covered up
with green and pink thread. I didn't think we'd *ever*
get that mess cleaned up.

Tou Vue and I were kind of hoping that our gift
would be an even bigger hit.

"I expect you sailors to behave in that store,"
Bobby's mom said as we piled into her Bronco.

Ms. Samson is younger than Moms, maybe by a
few years. She used to be in the Navy, and Bobby was
even born on an island—way out in the middle of the
Pacific Ocean. She has a picture of herself in uniform
on the wall in their house. It is a white uniform with
decorations and a bunch of gold. In another picture
she stands in front of a man in a uniform—a white
man, and his uniform is a dark color. There is another
picture of him by himself. He may be Bobby's father,
but none of us Wildcats really know. He *looks* like
Bobby, except Bobby really doesn't look white.
Bobby's hair *is* sort of curly—where mine is tight—

and his nose *is* sort of different from mine. And, come to think of it, Alf does sometimes look like a little white kid with a really good tan.

One time Johnny Vang asked Bobby if the man in the picture was his dad.

"Maybe," he said, and he shrugged.

I asked Moms where Mr. Samson is. She sort of knows Ms. Samson from the grocery store and the PTA.

"At sea, I imagine," she said. She said it the way that mothers say things when they know a good secret and they really, really, really want to tell you, but it isn't something you're supposed to talk about in front of kids.

Ms. Samson buckled Alf into his car seat. The other Alf sat next to her. The Wildcats rode in the back.

"I've got four items on my list," she said. "You landlubbers have 20 minutes. I'm shoving off at 1600, whether you're there or not." Bobby's mom is forever talking that Navy stuff.

We took off at a trot.

"Y'all still getting that Super Soaker?" Bobby asked. We ran down the aisle past the deodorant and the personal hygiene products. Tou Vue picked up a package of adult diapers and tossed it to Bobby.

"Don't forget these," he said. A woman gave us a dirty look, so we hightailed it out of there.

"Tell me something," I said to Bobby. "If your

mom was in the Navy and everything, what's she got against guns? They've got guns in the Navy, don't they?"

Bobby threw his hands in the air and rolled his head around like it had come loose. "You tell me," he said. "You know how mothers are."

We all nodded. We all know how mothers are.

The Super Soakers came in many different sizes and colors. The one we really wanted had a giant backpack-thing attached that you filled up with water—it carried like a million gallons of extra water. The gun had a double-barreled, dual-action hose, so you could fire short blasts of water or long streams. Get one of those babies, and people'd be begging for mercy. It cost over $30!

We settled for a much smaller one—one with a lime green tank that held five gallons of water. The price tag read $12.95, and after tax I'd still have enough money to buy something in the candy aisle for me and a card for Gumma Jackson. I had already made her a clay ashtray in art class. Gumma doesn't smoke, but she will love it anyway.

Gumma doesn't allow me to buy her presents. She says she has everything she could ever want in the world, including a precious grandson. What's a guy to do? Usually I bring her something anyway—a picture I made at school, a jewelry box, one of those smelly packages of powder that has a ribbon tied around it. I sneak them up on her so she is surprised.

Bobby had a $20 bill to buy his gift with, but he said that Ms. Samson expected some change.

I reached in my pocket and dug out a few quarters. "This could be some change right here," I said.

"And she didn't say how much change," Bobby added. He rolled his head around some more in that goofy way he has.

"You guys are very bad," Tou Vue said, but he smiled and nodded when he said it to let us know he was in with us all the way.

We wandered up and down the shelves of educational toys.

Eek! Boring!

There wasn't one thing in there a guy would want. A real guy, that is. One of those guys who is always trying to make points with the teacher or with his mom and dad, maybe. But not a real guy. Real guys want stuff you can throw or hit or shoot or jump on.

We went and looked at the sporting goods. Boy, was that stuff expensive! You wouldn't think a simple thing like a baseball glove would cost that much money. And, anyway, Tony R already had all that junk, he and his dad being sports freaks and all.

Bobby decided to buy a game. We found one of those that looked kind of silly and not too dumb. It was one of those games where you stacked up a bunch of mismatched pieces until they fell over. The person who put the last one on before the tower fell was the loser. The game looked okay, and we figured if it was boring, we could always use the pieces for ammo.

We added up our change. Bobby is the math whiz. It turned out we had enough left over to get a bag of Now-n-Laters and still give Bobby's mom some change. Then we headed out of the store.

"Does AWOL mean anything to you sailors?" Ms. Samson stood by her Bronco, tapping on her watch and giving us her best fake mean-mom face.

"Sorry," Bobby said. He dropped a handful of coins into his mother's outstretched hand. About $1.50. He made a goofy face and did more head rolling.

"Humph, humph, humph," she said, shaking her head.

None of us boys said anything at all. We all had a mouthful of Now-n-Laters. Because we were having such a good time, we even gave one to Alf, but we had to take the paper off first. Those little kids—their fingers don't work right yet. Alf smacked on his Now-n-Later. Some yellow drool leaked out of his mouth.

Bobby suggested we leave our presents in the clubhouse, but Ms. Samson said that wasn't a very good idea. She reminded us that some of the bigger kids liked to break into those sheds and steal things.

She said she would keep them for us until the party Saturday since Tony R lives down the block. I was glad not to have to lug the Super Soaker all the way home.

"You gentlemen will be wrapping these gifts, I hope," Ms. Samson said when we'd lugged in our packages.

We looked at one another. None of us had even thought about that. Before we could answer, she pulled out a bunch of silver paper she had bought, found some tape and some scissors, and told us to look lively.

We made sort of a mess. The paper got kind of crinkly and torn around the edges. It was hard wrapping that big gun!

"You call this a regulation corner?" Ms. Samson asked. "Watch this." She peeled off our paper, rewrapped the gifts, and made our presents look terrific.

"I hope you men paid attention," she said. "Next time you're on your own, and I expect those presents to be top-drawer."

We all laughed. We stopped when she told us that anyone who laughed was getting KP.

"All ashore that's going ashore," she said, opening her door. That meant it was time for Tou Vue and me to leave. It was on the way home that I got my best idea of all time to save me from the gummas.

"Buddy!" I said to Tou Vue, putting my arm across his shoulder. "Pal!"

"Uh-oh," Tou Vue said. "You're starting the buddy pal stuff. It must be trouble."

"What are you doing Saturday afternoon, old buddy, old pal?" I rubbed my hands together to let him know that there was real big fun in front of us.

"I don't know what I'm doing on Saturday," Tou Vue said. "But I don't think I'm gonna like it."

The One Gumma

"PUT THAT PAPER towel in the trash, Larry," Moms said. "Here comes that woman now."

Moms always gets this way whenever Gumma Underwood comes over. She had spent two days cleaning the house, with me helping her as much as she'd let me. The good thing about Gumma Underwood's visits is that Moms is so nervous, she feels like she has to do everything herself. The bad thing about Gumma Underwood's visits is that Moms goes a little crazy, and you can never even have a paper towel in your hand.

Pops had picked up Gumma Underwood, and she

was heading for our door. Pops was right behind her.

"Did you hear what I said, Wilton?" Gumma Underwood demanded.

"I heard you, I heard you, I heard you!" Pops said. He flew past me and Moms like we weren't even there, waving his hands like he was surrendering.

"Some people and their attitudes," said Gumma Underwood. "Slam a door in a person's face. Wilton! Wilton Underwood! I don't know what makes him think I won't spank him. I don't care how old that boy is."

"Nice to see you, Mother Underwood," Moms said. She had a look on her face as if Jack the Ripper had just walked in the room. She tried to cover it up with a smile.

"All I said to the boy was that a person didn't like to be kept standing on the street corner for hours and hours. Not in these times." Gumma Underwood pulled the pin out of her little black hat. The hat was covered with what looked like a bug net from science class. She set it on the table and kept right on talking. "You know how it is out there, Lorraine. Muggers and thieves and purse snatchers on every corner."

"I was ten minutes late," Pops shouted from the other room. "I told the woman I got caught in traffic. Ten minutes." If you listened carefully, you could hear Pops mumbling some things in the other room.

"Why don't you have a seat, Mother Underwood." Moms pulled out a chair from the kitchen table for her. She did it like she was afraid Gumma would bite her.

"Thank you, baby. I need to sit down. Hours and hours I stood there. You have no idea."

I heard my father make a sound like someone just punched him in the gut.

"Lorraine!" Gumma Underwood said, scuffing her feet on the linoleum. "When was the last time you washed this floor? It's getting kinda sticky in here."

Moms' smile now looked more like she was a wolf getting ready to bite somebody. She grabbed my arm and pinched me.

"Ouch!" I said.

"Get Gumma some ice water, Larry. I'll go help your father finish packing."

Then I could hear them both in the other room sighing.

"Don't just stand there! Come give Gumma some sugar!"

I tried to lean over and give her a little peck, but she snagged me like I was a big lunker and pulled me in. She wrapped her arms around me and gave me one of those big, juicy, slobbery kisses all over my face.

"Lord! Such a handsome and precious boy. Grandma'd like to eat you up."

"I'm supposed to get you some ice water," I said. I could hardly say it because she was strangling me.

She let loose, and I fell out of her arms onto the floor. The floor felt clean and smooth. Moms had spent all day scrubbing it.

"You poor, poor thing," Gumma said. "Left all alone in a dangerous city. Parents running off all over the country like crazy folks."

Gumma talked real loud, so I could tell it was not for my benefit. I handed her some ice water. She took a sip and set down the glass.

"Some woman has a baby. So what?" continued Gumma. "Is that a reason to run off and leave a defenseless child? You didn't see me abandoning my children for the weekend. Of course, I wasn't one of these modern mothers."

Moms marched into the kitchen behind Gumma with her hands out in front of her like the Frankenstein monster. There was gonna be trouble. Moms was gonna strangle Gumma!

Pops grabbed Moms by the shoulder and headed back in the other direction. He came back into the kitchen, pounded on the table three times, and then pointed at Gumma Underwood. He shook me gently and made a growling noise in the back of his throat. Then he turned around and left.

"Your father has always been emotional," Gumma said. "Even when he was a baby. I thought for a time there we were gonna have to put him on nerve pills. He grew out of most of it. MOST OF IT!" She said the last part really, really loud.

"I'll be right back," I said. I went to my parents' bedroom. "Can I help you guys with anything?"

I could hear Gumma's voice way back there at the other end of the house.

"I did my best," she said. "I tried to set a good example. For all the good it did."

Moms was lying across the bed like she'd fainted, fanning herself and cringing every time Gumma opened her mouth.

"Get back there and entertain your dear, sweet grandmother," Pops ordered, turning me around.

"Hey! I'm just a kid!"

"Here." He opened his wallet. "Here's a 20. There's more where that came from. Now get back there."

I went back to the kitchen.

"Hi, Gumma," I said.

"Thought I'd been abandoned," she pouted. "But what's a person to expect around here."

I was desperate. "I caught a frog today," I told her. "A bunch of us boys—the Wildcats—we went down to Crosby Park where there's always a whole bunch of frogs if you know where to look. Johnny Vang's keeping the frog at his house for the weekend."

"The Wildcats, huh," said Gumma suspiciously. "Sounds like a gang to me."

"It's not a gang. It's a club," I replied.

"I didn't let my children play with reptiles," Gumma said real loudly.

26

Moms let out another loud sigh from the bedroom.

"Frogs are amphibians, Gumma," I informed her.

A few minutes later Moms and Pops hustled by with their luggage. They were moving faster than people in those old silent movies.

Pops laid a fast kiss on Gumma's cheek and told her not to get up. She didn't.

I followed them out to the car.

"Hallelujah!" Moms said, raising her arms in the air.

Pops said, "Don't call us. We'll call you." They blew me a bunch of kisses, burned rubber out the driveway, and were gone.

I went back inside to Gumma. She sighed. "I thought they'd never leave."

She poured her glass of water into the sink, went into the living room, and sat in front of the TV.

"Go back in that icebox and get me one of them beers," she ordered. "Wipe off the top real good. A person can't be too careful, if you know what I mean."

The fun had begun.

Dinner for Three

GUMMA UNDERWOOD GOT the remote control and started flipping from channel to channel. She'd let the TV stay on one station for maybe ten seconds before she flipped it to the next one. She kept complaining that there was nothing on.

She stopped when she got to MTV.

"All right, now," she said, and started rocking back and forth to the music. "This is one of my *favorite* numbers."

"You like rap music, Gumma?" I asked.

"Gumma's down with all the latest sounds," she said, snapping her fingers.

I kinda liked that song too. We sat on the couch and bobbed our heads in time to the music.

"Whoop! There it is!" Gumma sang along with the rappers. Gumma was wearing old lady clothes so it was doubly surprising to see her enjoying Tag Team. She had on one of those old lady dresses that is real long and has flowers all over it and lace at the neck. She even had on those old lady black shoes that are real sturdy-looking. I was afraid of those shoes. I bet if she stepped on your foot, she would break your toes.

"Gumma," I said. "I think you kinda made Moms and Pops mad before they left."

28

Gumma made a farting noise with her lips. "I ain't studying Wilton and Lorraine," she said. "Coupla old fuddy-duddies."

"Moms and Pops are *not* fuddy-duddies," I said. At least I didn't think they were. I wasn't really sure what a fuddy-duddy was. "Moms and Pops are cool." For a mom and pop they are.

"Wilton and Lorraine like to think just 'cause he's working for the bus company and 'cause she's working for the school district that they know everything. I just like to bring 'em down a peg or two."

"That's mean, Gumma!" I exclaimed.

"Oh, mean my foot," Gumma said. "You telling me you don't like to tease folks now and then? I bet there's a couple of girls 'round here you don't mind teasing. Uh-huh. Yes, there are."

Actually it is kind of fun to tease Jenny Pedersen. She is a girl over on the next block who is in our class and who wants to be a Wildcat. She doesn't know the meaning of the words "no girls allowed."

Sometimes when we camp out in Tony R's backyard, we sneak next door to Jenny's house and make scary faces in her window with our flashlights. If we find big spiders, we leave them on her windowsill. They usually crawl away before she opens the window. She pretends to be scared, but really she isn't. She likes spiders and all kinds of bugs and crawly things. She screams, but that's just pretend. Then she gets out her sack full of water balloons to bomb us with. She keeps them handy just in case, and she really has a good aim. She is the best pitcher in our class. Jenny is Korean, and she was adopted. She doesn't take stuff from anyone. She always gets you back, even when you least expect it.

"Don't you worry about your momma and daddy," Gumma said. "They can take care of themselves. Gumma's just messing with them, all right?" Gumma rubbed my head.

"All right," I said, though the look in her eyes told me she was probably messing with me too.

We watched some more videos and then the doorbell rang.

"Tell 'em we don't want any," Gumma said, pushing me up from the couch.

"Yo, what it is," Johnny Vang said. He was on his in-line skates and had his hockey stick. "What's it doing, bro?"

Johnny Vang had moved to St. Paul when he was five. He was born in a refugee camp. Deep down inside, Johnny Vang wants to be a black person. He always talks like us. Well, not like us, actually, since I am us, and *I* don't talk like Johnny Vang. Johnny Vang talks *down*, like the kids in Chicago or like kids in the tougher parts of St. Paul. I could talk that way if I wanted to, but Moms and Pops don't like it. And it's too much trouble going back and forth. Me, I stick with regular old going-into-sixth-grade English, if you know what I mean.

"You down for some street hockey?" Johnny Vang asked.

Before I could explain that I had company, Gumma threw open the door and asked, "Who's this?"

"This is Johnny Vang, Gumma."

"Yo, what it is, Grams," said Johnny Vang.

"He's kind of a skinny thing . . . Oh, that reminds me," Gumma took off on a run for the kitchen.

"Why you call Grams 'Gumma'?"

Oops. I try to remember to say *Grandma* in front of people outside the family. I have called both Grandmas "Gumma" since I learned to talk. *Grandma* is kind of a hard word for a little guy to get his tongue around. I know it sounds stupid and I know I'm too old for it, but it's like a bad habit I need to break and haven't quite figured out how yet. And I wouldn't want to hurt Gumma's feelings or anything.

"That's her name," I told Johnny Vang. "Gumma."

I could see the confusion in his eyes, even behind his sunglasses. He shrugged and said, "Whatever."

Gumma Underwood came running back with her purse. "Y'all got one of them Chinese restaurants around here anyplace?" she asked Johnny Vang. She said it real loud, and I was so embarrassed, I could have died.

We walked over to Sibley Plaza where there is a Vietnamese restaurant. Johnny Vang came with us. I didn't remember inviting him. He sort of invited himself. He changed into shoes and took Gumma's arm. He gave her a tour of the neighborhood, telling her who lived in all the houses and anything exciting that had ever happened, like a fire or a car wreck or the police being called. I could see Gumma making a list of all those terrible things and then teasing Moms and Pops about them when they came home.

Gumma took one look inside the Vietnamese place and announced that it would do just fine. She sat on one side of the table, and we sat on the other.

"What's good here?" she asked Johnny Vang. I wished I could explain to her that, first, Johnny Vang wasn't deaf so there was no reason for her to shout, and second, that Johnny Vang was Hmong, not Vietnamese. How would he know what to eat in this restaurant?

Much to my surprise, Johnny Vang was full of advice.

"The hot and spicy chicken is slammin' in this joint," he said.

We ordered a bunch of food and then Gumma ordered a beer. She looked at the other customers.

"Kinda dead in here, ain't it?" Gumma said.

We boys just shrugged. It seemed pretty lively to me. There were four other tables with customers, and people were coming in and out for carryout. The restaurant *was* quiet, though. You could hear people's forks scraping across their plates.

"Y'all got a jukebox in here?" Gumma asked the waiter. He wasn't even at our table. He was across the room waiting on some other people.

The waiter turned around and shook his head. He pointed to a speaker. If you listened real hard, you could hear some quiet music playing—harps and bells and guitars, from what I could tell.

"Turn it up!" Gumma shouted.

"Yeah, pump up the volume!" Johnny Vang added.

The waiter did, but the music was so tinkly, it didn't make much difference.

"This the kind of music you all like over there in China?" Gumma said.

"What you talking, Grams? Johnny Vang not from China. Johnny Vang from the hood! Johnny Vang like rap, funk, all that good music!" said Johnny Vang.

Gumma and Johnny Vang gave each other a high five. Our food came, and we started eating.

"I bet you boys didn't know I was a fashion model," Gumma said. She patted her brownish red hair with her hands. I was pretty sure it was a wig, but it was hard to tell. It looked natural, but it also looked exactly the same way every time you saw her.

Johnny Vang and I tried to hide our faces. We were giggling.

"Nothing funny about that," Gumma said. "You can ask anybody. Loretha Watson was the prettiest thing this side of New York City. Yes, I was." Gumma took a sip of her beer, belched, and got up. Then she walked back and forth across the restaurant, like she was at a fashion show. Johnny Vang and I put our hands over our mouths.

"What are you looking at?" Gumma said to the people at one of the other tables. "If you took a picture, it would last longer." She came back and sat down.

"I had to give up my modeling career when I got married. One of these days I'm thinking about getting back in it."

Johnny Vang and I excused ourselves to the bathroom. We had both drunk two big pops. We went into the bathroom and laughed and laughed until I almost threw up.

"Your grams is crazy!" Johnny Vang said.

We would have fallen on the floor laughing, but the bathroom was kinda dirty-looking.

The waiter had left the check at our table. Gumma held it up in our faces.

"Who's paying for this?" she asked.

The bill said $18.

I looked at Johnny Vang and he looked at me. Neither of us had any money.

"Waiter!" Gumma called. "Better get these two started washing up the dishes. You boys hurry home when you're done."

"Some people think they can eat for free," Gumma announced to the whole restaurant. She pointed to us, walked out, and left us there!

The waiter came over with his hands on his hips

and a very stern expression on his face.

"Oh, no!" said Johnny Vang and put his head in his hands.

"Eek!" I said.

The waiter cracked a smile and then pointed us to the door with his thumb. Gumma had her face pressed to the glass, making faces.

"She already paid," the waiter laughed. We ran for the exit.

Gumma met us outside the door. She was jumping up and down, waving her fists and cackling.

"I got you! I got you!" she shouted. She wrapped her arms around us both and gave us a big hug. Good old Gumma. The people in the restaurant stood in the window and clapped for her. She took a deep bow.

We got ice cream from the supermarket for dessert and ate it in front of the Friday night TV shows. Johnny Vang skated off home, and Gumma and I got settled in for bed.

"Another day of fun and adventure ahead!" Gumma announced, kissing me good night.

I couldn't wait. We had had so much fun, I had completely forgotten about Gumma Jackson.

Boy was that a mistake!

The Other Gumma

ONE OF MY favorite things about Gumma Underwood is the way she likes to sleep in. When I stay over at her house, sometimes we sleep so late we miss lunch.

That is why when the doorbell rang on Saturday morning, it woke me up.

"Laaarrrrryy," Gumma Underwood called softly.

I put on my bathrobe and stopped in her room. The doorbell kept ringing. Gumma Underwood had her eyes closed and was turned to the side and balled up in the covers. I could barely see her in there.

"Get the door, baby," she said in a very groggy voice. "And don't let no strangers in the house." I turned around to leave but then jumped back in fright.

There was another Gumma Underwood!

But no. It was just her wig. It was on the dresser top on one of those fake heads, and it was covered with curlers. I patted it and went to see who was so impatient.

I peeked out the front door.

Eek! It was Gumma Jackson!

She pushed her way in and snatched me up in a hug.

"Thank goodness, you're all right," she said, squeezing me like she was a big snake. "I was on my way to summon the police. What was I to think?"

Gumma Jackson gave me a different kind of big kiss than Gumma Underwood. Where Gumma Underwood's kisses are wet and sloppy, Gumma Jackson's are fast, greasy smooches pecked all over my face like she is a chicken or something. I knew when I looked in the mirror I would find bright red lip marks all over my face.

"I thought you'd be up and dressed for our big day. Today's Gumma's thirty-ninth birthday!"

I thought last year was Gumma's thirty-ninth birthday. Come to think of it, so was the year before. If Moms was thirty-two and Gumma was only thirty-nine . . . it just didn't add up.

"Who's there, baby?" Gumma Underwood asked. She shuffled into the room, rubbing the sleep from her eyes.

"Well, if it isn't Loretha Underwood." Gumma Jackson crossed her arms on her chest.

"Cordelia Jackson. Over here and waking folks up at all hours of the night." Gumma Underwood pulled her robe around her and put a hand on one of her hips.

"For your information," said Gumma Jackson, "it's 10:30 in the morning. Decent people have been up and have already taken care of most of their business for the day. My grandson and I have an appointment, don't we, sugar?"

"Today's Gumma Jackson's thirty-ninth birthday!" I announced.

"Thirty-nine!" said Gumma Underwood. "That must be in dog years."

"Now you see here, Loretha Underwood . . ." Gumma Jackson started.

"Don't be pointing no fingers in my face . . ." Gumma Underwood continued.

I stepped between them and covered my ears to drown out the noise.

"Time-out!" I yelled, making a *T* sign in both of their faces. They both stopped and then looked at me like I was crazy. Usually when people call "time-out" they have something to say, but I didn't. I just stayed in the middle of them and kept making the *T*. The doorbell rang again.

It was Tou Vue. He did a little bow, and I let him in.

"Who is this?" both gummas asked.

"This is Tou Vue," I said. "He doesn't speak or understand any English."

Tou Vue smiled and nodded at each of the gummas.

"What's he doing here?" Gumma Underwood asked.

"My grandson can have company in his home if he wishes," Gumma Jackson said to Gumma Underwood. Then she said to me, "Lawrence, why is that child here?"

"His parents had an emergency," I said. "They asked if he could stay here."

"Wilton and Lorraine didn't say nothing about this," Gumma Underwood said.

"Oh . . . well . . . his parents don't speak English, either."

The gummas gave each other suspicious looks. Then Gumma Underwood started smiling.

"Lawrence, take your little friend and go get dressed so we can get started on our day."

Tou Vue started walking to my room before I did. I made a note to myself to remind him that since he supposedly didn't speak English, it might be better if he waited until I gave him the cue.

Gumma Jackson gave Gumma Underwood what Pops calls a perched-mouth look. She stuck her lips out real far and turned them to the side.

"What are you looking at?" Gumma Underwood asked her.

"Your hair looks so pretty like that," Gumma Jackson said.

Gumma Underwood gasped and felt her stocking cap. The wig was still back on the dresser! She stormed to the guest room and closed the door.

"Hurry up, Lawrence," Gumma Jackson said, "before that woman gets back out here."

"I heard that!" Gumma Underwood shouted.

From my room I could hear Gumma Underwood slamming closets and grumbling about Gumma Jackson. I thought I heard her mumble some things that I'm not allowed to repeat.

"Your grannies don't get along too good," Tou Vue said.

"That's an understatement."

"What's understatement mean?" he asked.

I had to think about it a minute. *Understatement* is one of those words you always hear people say and you sort of know what it means, but you can't really explain it to another person.

"Understatement is like . . . I think it's like you saying that my gummas don't like each other, when really it's like if we don't get Gumma Jackson out of here fast, they're liable to kill each other."

"Oh," said Tou Vue. "It means they really, really, really, *really* don't like each other. Like my Aunt Shoua and Cousin Yia."

"That's it," I said.

"Lu, is this gonna work today?" Tou Vue asked.

Another brilliant Lu Underwood creation: how could it *not* work! The plan was that with Tou Vue along, I wouldn't be stuck spending the day wandering around a bunch of old lady stores with Gumma Jackson. Whenever it got boring, I could make up the excuse that Tou Vue had to go to the bathroom or something like that. He and I could sneak off and play some video games or something. Then, when it got close to party time, if Gumma still wasn't done shopping, Tou Vue could fake being sick. Then we'd be at the party in plenty of time for the first taco. It was foolproof!

"Just remember," I told Tou Vue, pulling a clean Twins T-shirt over my head, "you can't understand anything she says to you. Just nod your head and smile."

He nodded his head and smiled.

"Just like that," I told him. "It's not so hard, is it?"

"Just like being in kindergarten," he said.

I grabbed a few quarters for the video machines at the mall, and we charged out to meet Gumma Jackson.

"Let's go," she said.

"Hang on just a cotton-picking minute," Gumma Underwood said. She had put on her blue pantsuit and plopped her wig back up on her head. "Just where do you think you're going, young man?"

"My grandson and I are going out to celebrate my birthday," Gumma Jackson said. "And if you don't believe it, you can get on the phone to *my* daughter who arranged it and check for yourself."

Gumma Underwood pointed her finger at Gumma Jackson again. "Well, *my* son told *me* that I was to be responsible for *my* grandson until he got back from Milwaukee. *My* son told *me* not to let this child out of *my* sight."

"Ooooh," Gumma Jackson seethed. "Loretha Underwood . . ." She put her hands on her hips and leaned forward.

So did Gumma Underwood. Tou Vue looked back and forth from one to the other. He looked like he was waiting for them to pull their guns from their holsters and start shooting. They looked like they just might do that. I had to stop this!

"It *is* Gumma Jackson's birthday," I said in a quiet and timid voice. "We always go somewhere. She and I do."

"That's right, Lawrence, and we were just on our way." Gumma Jackson grabbed my hand and started for the door. I grabbed Tou Vue.

"Fine, then," Gumma Underwood said. "Make room for me. I told my son I wouldn't let this child out of my sight, and Loretha Underwood is a woman of her word."

Gumma Jackson steamed out to the car with her red fingernails digging into my arm. "If you're coming, you'd better hurry up!" she yelled to Gumma Underwood. And then she started talking to me, but I could tell she really wasn't talking to me at all. She was sort of rambling. "You sit in the front by me, boys," she said. "She can set her ornery self in that backseat with her knees up in her face for all I care. I don't know who she thinks she's messing with. She better hurry her ugly-wigged self on out here."

"I heard that!" Gumma Underwood yelled.

Tou Vue bit his lip to keep from laughing.

It was gonna be a long day. (And that was an understatement!)

Get the Picture

FOR HER FIRST birthday treat, Gumma Jackson
wanted to go to an art museum in Minneapolis. It was
a real fancy place that didn't look like a museum at all.
It didn't have big columns out front, and there
weren't many statues of naked people inside. It looked
more like an office or a bank than anything else.

We parked on the other side of a park that had
sculptures in it. Gumma Jackson threw open her car
door, jumped out, and stalked into the garden. You
would have thought they were giving away free stuff
over there.

Gumma Underwood moaned and creaked open
her door. She stood up, and I saw that there was a
curler still stuck in the back of her wig.

"This cheap car's about got me crippled," she
complained. She staggered forward like her legs
wouldn't bend.

The gummas and Tou Vue and I stopped and
looked at a sculpture that had a cherry in a spoon and
a fountain coming out of it. It was really neat. It
made me wonder who came up with such an idea and
how it was made. Maybe the Wildcats could make
something like it for Crosby Park. We were a pretty
creative bunch. We could do it.

When we got close to the art museum, Gumma Jackson rushed toward the door. She stopped and sighed and turned around to wait for Gumma Underwood, who was taking her own sweet time, walking as if her legs hurt real bad. For a while there it looked like she would hardly make it.

Funny thing was, the night before, Gumma Underwood had walked just as well as Johnny Vang and me—had even run across Fort Road in front of a speeding car.

"Don't worry about me," Gumma Underwood said. "You children go on and enjoy yourself. I'll be fine."

Tou Vue and I followed Gumma Jackson into the lobby. It was modern in there just like the outside, with brightly colored mobiles hanging from the ceiling. Just before Gumma Underwood caught up with us, a guard asked us if he could help us find anything.

"No, thank you," Gumma Jackson said. "We're just waiting for that old lady back there."

After hearing that, Gumma Underwood straightened her back and remembered how to walk like a normal person. We didn't have to wait for her again.

The museum turned out to be kind of a cool place. It didn't just have a lot of pictures of trees and boats and things on the wall like I expected. It had strange things too. There was a giant electrical plug—

the kind you stick into the wall—except it was made out of cloth and was soft-looking and bent where the prongs were. On the floor in one room was a sled with a blanket and a piece of ham on it. And in another corner there was a dress made out of meat.

Meat! Who would have thought of that? And why?

"Hey, Lu. There's some pretty creepy stuff in here," Tou Vue whispered.

"Shhhh!" I put my fingers to my lips. It was quiet in the museum, and I knew from experience that my gummas could hear a pin drop in a football stadium.

It wasn't all creepy stuff in there. A lot of it was just different. A lot of it made you think. I tried to imagine what the artists who made these things were like. Where did they come up with their ideas? I also wanted to know why the museum decided to show these things and not some other things. If I brought my sled over and gave it to them, would they put it on display? I'd throw in the ham for free.

The museum was packed with cool people—lots of people in cool clothes and guys with goatees and dreadlocks and girls with weird colors of hair, just like on MTV. Gumma Jackson fit right in. Well, she almost did.

Gumma Jackson may be as old as Gumma Underwood, but she isn't an old retired gumma at all. She still has a job in a bank, and she wears real pretty clothes made of silk and hangs a lot of scarves around her neck. She has her hair done up like Patti

LaBelle's, so that it stands up all over her head. It has white and silver streaks in it, and it looks like some sort of black-and-white flower.

Gumma Underwood is the retired lady. She doesn't wear the kind of clothes Gumma Jackson does. Pops says it's because she is old-fashioned, and that old-fashioned people like to wear old-timey clothes and not draw too much attention to themselves. Moms says it's because she is too c-h-e-a-p to spend money on herself like Gumma Jackson does. Moms always spells c-h-e-a-p, forgetting that I am practically in sixth grade these days. Moms says someone ought to tell Gumma Underwood to get rid of all of her 1960s bell-bottom pantsuits. (*Someone* means Pops.)

I looked around the museum and saw that Gumma Underwood actually fit in pretty well too. Some of the girls with the MTV hair had on bell-bottom outfits just like hers!

"What is this thing?" Gumma Underwood asked. She had stopped in front of a painting that took up a whole wall. At least, I thought it was a painting. It was covered with blobs of brown and green junk and had a bunch of rocks hanging off it. In the middle was an airplane propeller.

"Cool!" I said. Tou Vue nodded.

"Looks like somebody threw up on this," Gumma Underwood said.

Gumma Jackson gasped. "Thank goodness you children have adults who can influence you to

47

appreciate the finer things in life. This, for your information, is an artist expressing his innermost confusion at the state of our chaotic world."

"This," said Gumma Underwood, "is about to make *me* vomit."

"Well, why don't you go sit your uncultured self down someplace?"

"I might do just that."

Gumma Underwood and Gumma Jackson were talking real loud to each other. The museum guards started walking toward us. Fortunately, Gumma Underwood found a place to sit. I hoped it wasn't a piece of art she was sitting on.

"You boys come with me," Gumma Jackson said. She took us through the rest of the galleries and told us about all the pictures and things. Gumma Jackson was either very smart or very good at making things up. She seemed to know about every painting in there!

"This artist was inspired by the light outside her New York studio," Gumma said. She stepped back from the painting and walked to the side a few feet. She looked at it from five or six different angles, squinting her eyes and smiling.

"Exquisite!" she said.

"How'd you learn about all these paintings, Gumma?" I asked.

"Well, I read prodigiously, you know. I can't overemphasize the importance of a good education," she said.

"That's cool," I said.

Gumma walked on, and Tou Vue signaled me with his hands. He pointed to a sticker on the wall next to the painting. It said that the artist was inspired by the light outside her New York studio. There were stickers just like that one next to all the paintings.

Tou Vue rolled his eyes.

I shook my head. I guess a good education is always close by if you know where to look for it.

We ended up in the basement of the museum. Gumma Underwood caught up with us down there. We looked at photographs a lady had taken of her family. There was nothing unusual about them. I mean, it was just people doing everyday things, like sitting at the kitchen table, or standing by their cars. Still, there was something kind of nice about these pictures. On each picture the photographer told you who the people were and why the picture was important. The story was right there inside the frame. The story made you stop and look at the picture again and think some more about the people.

The people in the pictures were all black people like me. That was also nice.

Gumma Jackson and Gumma Underwood didn't have so much to say while we were looking at the photographs. They stopped and read each story and stayed a long time in front of each one. Tou Vue and I had already seen everything three times and been to the bathroom before they were done.

The pictures were good, I thought, but I didn't know why the gummas were taking so long. The gummas each found a few pictures that they stopped to look at for a long time. They sighed or shook their heads like they were sad. One time they stopped and looked at each other for a whole couple of seconds with their lips pinned closed.

It got kind of strange down there. And quiet too.

But quiet never lasts long with the gummas.

We made our way back to the lobby. Gumma Underwood stretched and yawned real loud, standing up on her toes and reaching for the ceiling. "Time for my nap," she announced.

"Pish," said Gumma Jackson, waving her hand at her. "Time for more fun, isn't it, boys? Who's hungry?"

I said, "Me! Me!" and Tou Vue jumped up and down. I thought it was okay that he did that because *hungry* is sort of a universal word anyway.

"Lunchtime, Loretha!" Gumma Jackson called. She gave Gumma Underwood a pleasant smile that underneath I could tell was kind of hateful too. Gumma Jackson practically ran to her car. Gumma Underwood walked behind her, imitating the way Gumma Jackson switched her behind when she walked.

Tou Vue and I laughed so hard we almost knocked over one of those sculptures in the garden. It was bronze, though, and heavy, so it was okay.

Jimmy Flopsweat's

WHEN WE GOT to the car, Gumma Underwood managed to get herself a front seat by moving me aside as soon as Gumma Jackson unlocked the doors.

"The nerve of some people," Gumma Jackson said.

Gumma Underwood turned around to us boys in the backseat. "You can tell some other people that if they think I'm riding around cramped up in the backseat of this sardine can, they've got another think coming."

Then Gumma Jackson turned around and said, "And you can tell a certain person, that, number one, if she doesn't like the transportation, she can walk, if her old legs still work. And number two, at least I have a car. Unlike some people."

Gumma Underwood gasped. "Why you!"

"I'm hungry!" I shouted. Both gummas gave me a dirty look, but at least they stopped their stupid argument.

Gumma Jackson started the car and asked us boys what we wanted to eat.

"What does your little friend like?" she asked.

"Tou Vue will eat anything," I said. "Pizza. Hot dogs. Pizza. Hamburgers. Pizza. Everything," I said.

Tou Vue nodded and smiled.

"Well, pizza might be okay," Gumma Jackson said. "All that grease and cheese, though."

"Yeah! Pizza," I said.

"Humph," Gumma Underwood said. "I guess that's some people's idea of nutrition."

"There's nothing wrong with pizza, Gumma," I said. "It has all your basic food groups. Sausage is your meat, cheese is your dairy, crust is your grains, and the mushrooms and stuff in the sauce are your vegetables."

I was sure glad I had paid attention during fourth-grade nutrition class.

"As much as I hate to say this, Lawrence," Gumma Jackson said (right then I knew we weren't getting pizza), "I think Loretha has a point."

The real problem with pizza is that it's one of those foods that gummas don't know how to eat.

They are afraid to pick it up because they might drop something on their clothes. And it's stupid to use a knife and fork when you eat pizza.

"Maybe we should choose something else," Gumma Jackson suggested.

Tou Vue snapped his fingers in disappointment. I nudged him with my elbow.

Gumma Jackson drove us to Jimmy Flopsweat's, this really great place out in the suburbs.

When you go in Jimmy Flopsweat's, the first thing you do is order your hamburger. They have three different sizes: the Big Daddy, the Mamaburger, and the Pup.

Gumma Jackson pointed to me and Tou Vue and herself. "I'm paying for these three," she said. She smiled at Gumma Underwood.

"We want Big Daddies," I said. Tou Vue nodded and smiled. "Make that Big Daddies, French fries, and two monster-sized pops," I said.

Gumma Jackson put in our order and ordered herself a Pup.

Gumma Underwood got up to the window and looked kind of confused. "What do I do here?" she asked.

"You just tell them what you want," I told her. "When it's done, they call you up to the window to get it."

"What *do* I want?" Gumma Underwood asked me.

I ordered for her. I got her the same thing Tou Vue and I had ordered.

While we were waiting for our food, we went over to the game area. There were video games, a basketball hoop, and a couple of skee-ball games. There were prizes for whoever got the top score. All the games had kids playing them, except for the skee ball, so Tou Vue and I tried it.

Skee ball is a kind of dumb game, really. All you do is toss these different-colored balls up a ramp. On top is a bull's-eye kind of thing, and you get points depending on which hole on the bull's-eye your ball falls into. It's a lot harder than it looks. I think it's rigged so that's it's almost impossible to win anything.

I played first. My first two balls didn't go into any holes at all. That was kind of embarrassing. But the good thing is that if the ball doesn't go in, it rolls back down and you get to shoot it over again. My third ball went into a 10-point hole.

Tou Vue got a 30-point hole on his first try.

After we had each rolled all 5 of our balls, I had 70 points and Tou Vue had 85 points. Rats! You had to have at least 100 to get even the cheapest prize. It wasn't so much that I wanted one of those pink plastic key rings, but a guy's got to have a little pride, doesn't he?

Gumma Underwood went up to the guy who ran the games and pulled out a dollar.

"Give me some more of those balls," she said.

Gumma Jackson looked like her feelings were hurt. She pulled out her own dollar.

"I'd like a set of those balls, as well," she said.

Eek! The gummas were going to have a skee-ball tournament!

Gumma Underwood picked up her first ball. Gumma Jackson watched her.

She massaged the ball between her two palms and blew air on it. "Come on, baby," she said.

She tossed that ball up there and right into the bull's-eye. Fifty points!

"Yes!" Gumma Underwood exclaimed. She put her hands on her hips and turned and looked at Gumma Jackson. Her look said she dared Gumma Jackson to do better.

Gumma Jackson set her purse down and picked up her red ball. She didn't blow on it or do any of the things Gumma Underwood had. She reared back her hand like she was ready to throw a pitch.

"No, Gumma!" I yelled. "Underhand!"

"Oh," she said. She tossed it up there like she was throwing a magazine onto a couch. She didn't aim or anything.

She got a 10-point hole. Just like my third ball.

"Heh, heh, heh," Gumma Underwood laughed. It was an evil-sounding laugh.

"You just wait," Gumma Jackson said.

By this time, a bunch of moms and dads and kids

were standing around watching us. I just hoped the gummas behaved themselves.

Gumma Underwood got ready for her next roll. She picked up a yellow ball and slathered it with some of her juicy kisses. The ball looked slobbery and sad. I knew how it felt.

"Come to Poppa!" she yelled, and threw it up there. She got a 10-pointer.

"Heh, heh, heh, yourself," Gumma Jackson said.

She threw her ball up there without any warning and got a 40.

The score was 50 to 60.

The two gummas battled it out just like those guys on the tournament of professional bowlers. After the fourth ball, the score was tied 110 to 110. Even the manager of Jimmy Flopsweat's had come over to watch. I hoped somebody was still cooking our food.

Gumma Underwood was giving Gumma Jackson what Pops calls her fish-eyed look. That's the one where she squints her eyes and purses her lips and looks like she is going to bite you. Gumma Jackson was leaning back against her skee-ball table, looking like a movie star, her head tossed back and her scarves trailing out behind her.

Gumma Underwood kissed her ball. "Don't fail me now!" she said. She pulled back her arm, let go, and BLAM!

Right into the 50-point hole!

"In your face, Cordelia!"

Gumma Jackson was cool. "Not so fast, granny," she said. "I got my lucky ball left." She had saved her black ball for last.

I don't think anyone in that place was breathing. I know I wasn't.

Gumma Jackson flipped one of her rainbow scarves back around her neck. She pinched her lips together in concentration, reared her arm behind her, and BLAM!

Right into the 50-pointer!

The restaurant exploded in applause.

The gummas had tied!

The gummas let us pick out the prizes. There wasn't anything good, unless you had at least 200 points, but we got two miniature troll dolls. I let Tou Vue take them home to his sisters.

When our names were called, we picked up our burgers. After you pick up your sandwiches, you go to a big salad bar area where you can put any kind of junk on them you want. That's the best thing about Jimmy Flopsweat's. I put relish and catsup and cheese sauce and onions and just a little bit of mustard on my burger. Tou Vue went straight for the hot peppers. He loaded up his burger with hot peppers and barbecue sauce. Yuk! To each his own is what Moms always says.

We went and sat down with our food. Three of us had humongous burgers and Gumma Jackson had a little tiny one.

"Yours looks kind of funny next to ours," I said to Gumma Jackson.

"Some of us like to maintain a petite figure," she said, and took the tiniest of bites.

Gumma Underwood took a long pull off of her pop and stared Gumma Jackson right in the eye.

"And some of us . . . no, some of us are gonna do the mature thing and enjoy our meal."

They stared at each other and chewed.

The war was hardly over. This was barely even a truce.

Shopping Spree #2

WE MANAGED TO finish our lunches without anything terrible happening. Both gummas ate their hamburgers quietly. They smiled at me and at Tou Vue and at the other customers. They didn't look at each other at all.

Before we left the restaurant, Tou Vue and I went to the bathroom for a meeting.

"Lu, it's really hard not to talk," Tou Vue said. "I think I almost bit a hole in my lip."

"You're doing great!" I said. "Hang in there."

I felt sorry for him, but I knew he would survive. Tou Vue usually didn't say much anyway.

"Only a couple more hours," I told him. "It's 2:30 now. Our goal is to be home no later than 4:00. We don't want to miss any of the party!"

He sighed and shook his head.

"We'll make it," I said.

"Yeah, but will your grandmothers make it?"

I said I didn't know. I was getting tired. It was hard being around people who didn't get along. I kept thinking that maybe if I did the right thing or said the right thing, they would act differently. Maybe they would get along and everyone would be happy. I knew that wasn't true.

THE GUMMA WARS

Some people just weren't meant to be around each other. Like Danny O'Brien, over on Eleanor Street. He likes Bobby okay, but he hates the rest of the Wildcats. We don't like him too much, either. When he is over at Bobby's house, we try to be nice to him, for Bobby's sake. Other than that, we stay away from him. Bobby always asks us to try to get along, but it doesn't do any good. Danny is mean, and he picks fights with people for no reason. He is just someone you'd rather not be around.

We left Jimmy Flopsweat's and headed over to Sandburg's Department Store. Sandburg's is a big building up in the Midway section of St. Paul. It is different from a lot of stores. For one thing, it isn't in a mall. Sandburg's just sits in the middle of a big parking lot, all by itself. It is *huge* inside and outside— *THREE BIG FLOORS*, its sign says. There is a big tower on top of the building, and at Christmas time, lights are strung all the way to the top.

"Now for my favorite part of *my* birthday!" Gumma Jackson said. "The time when *I* get to buy a gift for *my* grandson." She tossed her scarves behind her, grabbed my arm, and started for the entrance.

This is my favorite part of her birthday too. Ever since I can remember, Gumma Jackson has taken me to Sandburg's on her birthday and let me pick out something for myself. Moms tells her she is spoiling me and sending me all the wrong messages about gift giving. Gumma tells her that she is just jealous because she doesn't have a grandmother to buy her nice things whenever she wants to and just because she loves her. Moms gets so upset she can hardly talk.

"You just better enjoy that present, young man," Moms always says to me, " 'Cause that's one less you're getting on your own birthday!"

Not that Moms would actually hold out on me. Like I said, Moms and Pops are pretty cool for a mom and dad. And lucky for me, Moms is so busy with her job as school secretary she always forgets about Gumma's gift anyway.

I followed Gumma Jackson to the store and let my imagination take hold. Should I get a new video game? Or a new stereo headphone set? Maybe a pair of hockey skates—but, no, it was a long time until winter, and I wanted something I could use today!

Just as we entered Sandburg's, Gumma Underwood said, "Just a second there, Cordelia."

"I thought we'd left you in the car," Gumma Jackson said.

"You don't need to get huffy. I just wanted to know how long you was gonna be."

"As long as it takes to find the perfect gift for *my* grandson. Come along, Lawrence."

"Did it ever occur to you that someone else might want to get *her* grandson a gift? You come on with your Gumma Underwood, Larry."

Eek! Two presents! And my birthday wasn't for

another three months. Having two gummas had its advantages.

"Lawrence," one gumma called.

"Larry," called the other.

"Lawrence!"

"Larry!"

"All right, already!" I said.

Having two gummas also had its *dis*advantages. I stood there feeling like a piece of taffy. Gumma Underwood had her hands on her hips and a smirk on her face. Gumma Jackson stood in her swirl of scarves. She had one of those sweet-looking smiles on her face like the evil ladies' smiles on *Heart and Home*—the soap opera my mom watches on her days off. When those evil ladies start smiling like that, you know there's gonna be trouble. I came up with an idea.

"Why don't we do this? First I'll go with Gumma Jackson. When we're done, Gumma Underwood can have me. Okay?"

"Let's get started, Lawrence," Gumma Jackson said. She smiled her evil soap-opera-lady smile at Gumma Underwood.

"I'll be looking for my grandson right here in exactly twenty minutes," Gumma Underwood said. "You hear me? Twenty minutes. And not one minute more."

Then Gumma Underwood really surprised me. She grabbed Tou Vue!

"I'm taking this one with me," she said. She grabbed my buddy and took off down the aisle. As he was dragged away, he looked back with big, desperate eyes.

"Where shall we begin?" Gumma Jackson asked me. "Let's pretend we've got this whole store to ourselves."

She hooked her elbow around my arm and started walking. I didn't know what to say. I was sad. I could have almost anything in the whole entire department store, but somehow shopping wasn't much fun anymore.

"Gumma Jackson," I asked, "why don't you like Gumma Underwood?"

"My goodness, Lawrence," she said. "What kind of question is that?"

"I don't know. It's just that you two argue all the time."

Gumma sighed and rearranged some of her scarves. "I'm not sure what to tell you, Lawrence. Let's just say that Cordelia and I have different ideas about things. I'm not sure she's *our* kind of people. If you know what I mean."

I *didn't* know what she meant. Gumma Underwood sure was *my* kind of people, I thought. She was fun and funny, and she loved me a lot. For that matter, Gumma Jackson was my kind of people too. That's what is sort of nice about the two gummas—how different they are. Just like Moms and

Pops are different. Pops is a guy who is mostly always in a good mood. If you get on his bus, he will always say good morning to you. He laughs with the riders and tells them jokes. He has the #12 run out of Roseville in the morning, and at Christmas, his regular riders bring him food and presents.

Moms is more serious, but more scatterbrained too. She is the sort of person who can never remember where she left anything. "Larry, did you move my purse?" she always asks me. Her purse is almost always where she left it—in the living room on the floor next to the TV.

So I have four adults around, and they are as different as north and south and east and west. I didn't see why Gumma Jackson thought that had to be a bad thing.

"We aren't going to let anything ruin our special day, are we, Lawrence?" she asked.

"I guess not." I was still sad.

"So, where shall we head?" Gumma asked. "We've got this whole store to pick from!" She spun around and her scarves spun out from her like a fountain.

While I was trying to decide, she said "Never mind" and took off running, pulling me behind her toward the escalator.

"I know just the place," she said.

We ended up on the third floor, where they keep all the stuff Moms likes—the sheets and towels and blankets and curtains. I was getting discouraged to

64

tell you the truth. I liked a nice, fresh towel, but as a present?

"Over here!" Gumma said. "Hurry up! We haven't got all day."

That was for sure. It was after 3:00, and I still had to shop with Gumma Underwood.

She took me to a section marked "Hobbies," and then I felt really discouraged. In the Hobbies department there was nothing but books for putting stamps in and books for putting coins in and pieces for model railroad sets.

"Let's see what we have here," Gumma Jackson said. She breezed up and down the aisles of paint-by-numbers sets and model car kits. I'm not exactly a model-cars kind of guy. Don't get me wrong. I think models are terrific, and if you go over to Kevin's house, you'll see he has every one of the models I saw at Sandburg's, and they're put together perfectly too. Each of Kevin's cars and planes has all the decals in exactly the perfect spot. When I try to build a model, the outside always ends up smeared with glue, and if there are supposed to be stripes on the wing, mine are always lopsided.

"So many fun things to do!" Gumma cheered.

I tried not to act disappointed. After all, it was her birthday, and it was her money. Still, a guy did kinda want to choose his own toys, and there was nothing worse than having to act like you really liked some dumb old present—like when Moms gives me a pair

65

of socks or some handkerchiefs. Maybe Moms was right. Maybe I was getting spoiled.

"I know just the thing," Gumma said. Now she had on her I-was-just-teasing-you look. She dragged me up to the counter. She pointed to a locked glass cabinet behind the cash register.

"My grandson and I would like to look at those," she said.

At first I thought she was pointing to this bird-watchers' catalog, but then I saw what she meant. A pair of binoculars!

"Ah!" the salesman said. "Madam has chosen our best pair." He handed them to me. He was a young guy who was probably still in high school. I thought it was weird for a guy like that to call Gumma "Madam."

The binoculars were heavier than I thought. The outside felt like leather, but I figured it was some kind of metal. I kept turning them around in my hands and looking at all the different parts. I thought of the great things I could do with those babies. I could go out to Crosby Park and look at all the boats up close. Or go over to Jenny Pederson's house and spy on her and her friends.

"Aren't you going to try them?" Gumma asked.

"Sure. How?"

"Like this." The salesman took the glasses and adjusted the binoculars to fit my face. They folded up sort of like a V. He showed me how to turn the eyepieces until things became clearer. I pointed the binoculars down the center of the aisle and started focusing. You'd never believe what I saw!

Into focus came Gumma Underwood storming down the aisle, dragging Tou Vue behind her.

"There they are!" she yelled. She had a whole handful of packages, and her wig had somehow gotten crooked. "Cordelia Jackson, your time is up!"

Gumma Jackson pouted. "We'll take these," she said to the salesman.

I didn't even get to see how much they cost. She put them on her charge, and then hung them around my neck.

Gumma Underwood gave my new binoculars a dirty look. "Some present," she said.

Gumma Jackson stuck her nose in the air.

"Come on, Larry," Gumma Underwood said. "Let's go find the fun part of the store." She dragged me away by the arm the same way she'd been dragging my buddy.

I signaled for Tou Vue to come with me. He shook his head and looked at me like I was being kidnapped by aliens. Gumma Jackson put a hand on his shoulder. I had the feeling she thought she was protecting him from something.

Shopping Spree #3

GUMMA UNDERWOOD WALKED with long strides.

She is an inch or two taller than Gumma Jackson, and maybe a little bit skinnier—it is hard to say. Gumma Jackson always wears clothes that flow around her body like she is swimming in them. Pops teases that she wears those clothes because she's so fat, but that makes Moms really mad. "Don't get me started on *your* mother's wardrobe," Moms always answers. That usually ends the discussion.

"Where's the toy department?" Gumma yelled to a salesclerk in the part of the store where they have the dishes.

"First floor, next to sporting goods," a lady answered. I could have told her that.

Gumma didn't even say thank you. She was in too big a hurry.

"That woman thinks she's gonna monopolize all my grandbaby's time," Gumma Underwood said. "No, ma'am. No, she's not. Acting all uppity and snooty. Thinks she's better than everybody else. I'll show her a thing or two. Yes, I will."

Gumma Underwood was not talking to me. She was talking to the air. Tou Vue told me later that she did the same thing the whole time he was with her too. He said it was really embarrassing. Worse than that, he said they spent the whole time in the *ladies' underwear department*! He said that Gumma Underwood went to every table that had ladies' panties on it and dug through them all three or four times. She kept complaining about how they never had anything in her size.

Tou Vue said people kept looking at him and wondering why he was following a crazy black lady around the underwear department.

"Then we went to the bras," he told me, shaking his head. I tried to get him to tell me more, but he refused. It must have been too gross. But, better him than me, I guess.

Like I was saying, Gumma was making a beeline for the toy department. She kept mumbling under her breath about Gumma Jackson. I thought it only fair to ask her the same question I'd asked the other gumma.

"Gumma, why don't you like Gumma Jackson?" I asked.

"What?" she asked, like I'd startled her. "Who said I don't like Cordelia?"

"No one," I answered.

"Better not. One thing I don't like is folks talking what they don't know."

I persisted. I was going to get to the bottom of this if it killed me.

"What I meant was, I was wondering why you're always saying things about her and arguing with her. That kind of stuff."

"Larry Underwood, I don't have the slightest idea what you're talking about," she said. She looked like she was insulted.

Then she said what she really meant. She said, "And I suggest a certain child keep his nose out of grown folks' business."

There. That was the whole thing right there. As far as Gumma Underwood and a lot of other grownups are concerned, kids are just dumb little people who don't know what's going on around them. Didn't she think I'd noticed she'd been angry all day? Didn't she think I could hear all the mean things she and Gumma Jackson said about each other? Of course I noticed! Of course I heard! What do people expect? That kids are just going to pretend nothing's happening? That kids don't care? I was getting tired of it, and I wasn't going to take it anymore.

"I don't want any more fighting between you and Gumma Jackson," I said. I said it with the same voice Pops uses when he has to yell at the Wildcats during basketball season.

Gumma made the farting noise with her lips again.

"Stop meddling," she ordered. She practically slung me into the toy department. "And start shopping!"

I got the message. And if a guy was gonna be punished, well, I guess this was the punishment to pick. I could just see myself on my knees begging after I'd made a mess in the kitchen at home. "Please, Moms, don't make me buy any more toys."

The only problem with Sandburg's is that it doesn't have a very good toy department. Not unless you're a little kid or a baby, that is. Sandburg's specializes in things like those stackable rainbow rings and xylophones and farm sets with wooden cows and sheep. There isn't much there for a guy my age.

"How much did *these* cost?" Gumma asked, snatching up the binoculars and almost pulling my neck off.

"I don't know," I said.

"No matter," she said. "Get whatever you want."

"Gumma, they don't really have much I want in this store," I said.

71

"How about this?" She held up one of those factories where you put in colored dough and mash out different shapes.

"That's a little young for me."

"This?" She held up a yellow-and-blue dump truck.

I shook my head.

We went up and down a couple of aisles doing that. Gumma would hold up something that was all wrong, and I would tell her so. Anything that was even close to being cool, I already had or one of the other Wildcats had, which meant there was no reason for me to buy another one. Most of our junk ends up at one another's houses anyway. If you want to borrow something, you just ask.

Gumma got real frustrated. She thought I was being a baby and being stubborn, and that I didn't want a present from her. What could I do? When you get to be my age, you already have a lot of junk, and these days most of the toys are pretty boring. Action figures from TV shows and junk like that. I already had enough action figures at home to last me the rest of my life.

Now if we were over at the Sports Shack, we'd be in business. I could just see Gumma dropping a wad of money on a new set of rookie cards. But we were at Sandburg's, and I didn't want to hurt her feelings. I also didn't want her to waste her money. The only aisle left was the Barbie aisle.

I looked across the store, and I got a brainstorm.

"I know what you can get me," I said.

Across the aisle was the electronics department. I saw the perfect gift for me. I led Gumma to the clock radios. I had been wanting one of these babies for the longest time, ever since Pops got his. He could set his so he woke up to his favorite sounds, and he could also set it so that it played sweet music until he fell asleep. It turned off all by itself.

"I think I'd like one of these," I said.

Gumma picked up the floor sample and looked it over. She nodded and smiled.

"Now we're getting somewhere," she said.

We searched the shelf until we found a box with the same serial number on it as the floor sample.

"This ought to show her," Gumma mumbled, rummaging through her purse looking for her wallet.

Just then, Tou Vue and Gumma Jackson found us.

"Oh, Lawrence! What a coincidence I found you here. I was just thinking I should get you one of these."

She picked up a CD from Two Bad Boys and 5— the latest rap group that everyone was so crazy about.

"No, you wasn't gonna get him that, 'cause I was," said Gumma Underwood. She grabbed another copy of the CD and stuck it in the flap of her purse while she continued fishing for her money.

"You get him that, Loretha, and I'll get him this." Gumma Jackson grabbed a CD by Desperation

Seekers, who are a cross between a heavy metal and a grunge band. Kevin has all their CDs, but I can't stand them.

"What I'd really prefer is this," I said, and I picked up the latest disc from Salina Salon. She sings these real mushy love songs, but they kind of grow on you. She is real pretty too. You should see her videos!

"Fine," Gumma Underwood said. She slammed my CD on the counter and paid the cashier.

"I think that's totally uncalled for," Gumma Jackson said. She seemed to be talking to Tou Vue when she said it. Gumma Underwood spun around.

"I've had about enough of you, Cordelia. I've been running up and down these streets with you all day long. Here it is 4:00 and . . ."

"Four o'clock!" I said. Eek!

Tou Vue's mouth dropped open.

"Hurry up, you guys," I ordered. "We'll meet you out by the car."

Tou Vue and I took off. We ran out the same door we had come in. I started down the closest row of cars, looking desperately for Gumma's car. It was almost time for the party, and we had to get out of there!

"Wait a minute," Tou Vue said. "I think your grandma's car is down that lane."

"I think it's down here."

"Let's go look," Tou Vue said, and I started to go, but then I suggested we wait for the gummas. If there's anything that makes gummas crazy, it's the thought of kids wandering up and down the lanes of parking lots and maybe being snatched or hit by a car. No matter that it would never happen in a million years. It's just the thought of kids and cars that makes them crazy. Mine were already crazy enough as it was.

"I hope they hurry," Tou Vue said. We were both so anxious to go, we paced back and forth in front of the door.

Finally, I could see them, headed in our direction. I could see through the glass that their lips were moving and that they were fussing with each other again. I figured their voices were real loud too.

Gumma Jackson pulled open one door and Gumma Underwood the other.

"You just would say something like that, wouldn't you?" Gumma Jackson said.

"Ha!" said Gumma Underwood.

They stormed right past us like they didn't even see us.

So did a man.

A man in a suit.

He was the store detective.

"Excuse me, ladies," he said, grabbing them by the elbows. "If you would step back inside for a minute. Please don't make this any harder."

Eek! And double eek!

The Big Breakout

"GET YOUR HANDS off of me!" both gummas yelled.

The store detective was a big strong-looking guy. He hauled them back into the store like they were nothing but rag dolls and plucked the unpaid-for CD out of the side flap of Gumma's purse.

"I can explain that," Gumma Underwood said. "I meant to pay for that. I got witnesses."

"I have nothing to do with this," Gumma Jackson said. "I have never seen this woman before in my life."

Some of the other customers stood around gawking at them. Some of them were laughing, but most of them just looked embarrassed. Like I felt.

"Wait!" I yelled, but I didn't yell it too loud.

The detective ignored me.

I followed them back into the store, but Tou Vue grabbed me and held me back.

"Don't get too close," he said. "They might arrest us too."

What a weekend this was turning out to be. I was going to be late to the best party of the year. Moms and Pops were out of town. Both gummas were under arrest. That meant almost everybody I was related to in the whole world was in the wrong place—including me!

We stayed about three or four shoppers behind the store detective, making sure we could keep the gummas in sight. Not that it was so hard. They were making such a ruckus, that everyone in the store had stopped to watch.

"I'm calling my attorneys," Gumma Jackson said.

"I'm calling the civil rights," said Gumma Underwood.

Boy, did they call that guy some names. Among the ones I can repeat are heathen, manhandler, lily-livered sapsucker, pasty-faced scoundrel, and ugly-suit-wearing no-account off-duty flat-footed fool.

The detective walked them through the paint department and then through a pair of metal doors. The doors swung closed behind them with a *whap*!

"What do you think they'll do to them back there?" I asked.

"I don't know," Tou Vue answered. "My cousin Show got picked up for shoplifting at the drugstore. I think they take you back there and yell at you a lot and then call the police."

I was glad he told me that. I had a picture in my head of a room with a mean-looking guy who talked with a funny accent. I pictured that he would beat the gummas with a length of rubber hose until he got them to confess to a big jewelry heist. I had been watching too many old movies on the cable channel.

Still, I was nervous.

"I think one of us should go back there and check on them," I said, pointing to Tou Vue.

"I don't think I like the sound of that," he said.

"If I went, they'd know right away who I was. But no one will suspect you."

"I was afraid you would say that," he said.

I pretended to search through the rack of paint samples. It was sort of fun actually. A person could choose from a whole rainbow of colors. You would never know this if you came to our house. All of our walls are white. Pops says white holds your home's resale value, whatever that means. Me, I'd prefer it if my room were one of these great shades of blue.

Tou Vue came zipping up the aisle and signaled me to follow him. We hid over by the tool department.

"Well? What's the deal?" I asked.

Tou Vue shook his head. "It's really sad," he said.

Oh no! It was the rubber hose after all.

"They're sitting in this tiny room right inside the door," he said. "They're both crying and blowing their noses and talking at the same time. The store guy is just standing there holding up the CD. He looks like he's gonna cry too."

"We've got to get them out of there," I said. The gummas were in trouble. And it was almost 4:30— the best part of the party could be happening right now! "We've got to think of a plan," I said.

At first we thought we'd do something crazy, like

take our clothes off and run around the store. Then we thought about stealing stuff, but we decided we'd probably just end up getting arrested too. Then we would never get to Tony R's party.

"Hey Lu! I think I got it!" Tou Vue said. We were wandering around the hardware department and the automotive department. I hoped his plan didn't include tools. I'm not too good with my hands.

"Look at this," Tou Vue said. He pointed to the emergency exit. The sign said WARNING: USE ONLY IN CASE OF EMERGENCY. ALARM WILL SOUND.

"I don't get it," I said.

"That's why I'm the brains around here," said Tou Vue.

I won't bore you with the brains' details. Let's forget the fact that there were probably people watching the two of us the whole time through hidden cameras. And the fact that if I really thought about it, I couldn't see either of my gummas making a break for the front door, even if a Hmong kid showed them the way. Let's just say that Tou Vue's plan was better than anything I'd come up with (which was nothing), and I was desperate. I wasn't missing that party for anybody.

My job was to stand by the emergency door. I had never been this nervous in my entire life. Springing your gummas out of the slammer was serious business. My palms were so wet, I could hardly hold my binoculars. I used them to watch for my signal from Tou Vue, who was down by the metal doors.

I saw him tip open one of the doors and signal, "Not yet." I looked at him through the binoculars again and saw his eyes getting really big. He was looking straight at me.

I felt a hand on my shoulder. EEK! It was another one of those store detectives, with a walkie-talkie and everything.

"Something I can help you find, young man?" the detective said. I barely heard him say it. I didn't even notice his big friendly smile.

I screamed and threw open the emergency door and ran out of there as fast as I could. I could hear the alarms ringing behind me as I ran.

Enough Is Enough

I RAN AROUND to the front of the store and hid out in the parking lot near where Gumma Jackson had parked her car. I don't know whether the walkie-talkie guy followed me or not. I was too scared to look back. I ducked down between cars, staying as close to the ground as possible. I listened for the sounds of sirens and police cars, but I didn't hear any. Eek! I'd really done it this time.

I got brave and stuck my head up. Nothing was going on. Cars drove around looking for spaces. Shoppers went in and out of the entrance. The store was going about its business as if nothing had happened!

I snuck a couple of cars closer. The door to the store opened, and out came Tou Vue with the gummas behind him. I ran over to him.

"The plan worked!" I yelled.

Tou Vue shook his head. "Actually, the detective just let them go."

The gummas had their arms crossed. They were both scowling.

"I thought you said this child didn't speak no English," Gumma Underwood yelled.

"I think you lied to us, Lawrence," Gumma Jackson said. "I do not like being lied to."

Tou Vue told me later that, even though he wasn't ready, as soon as I opened the emergency door, he went ahead with the plan. While all the security people ran to check out the alarm, he was supposed to bust out of there with the two gummas and head to the car.

"Instead, I met them coming out the door," he told me. "I told them to follow me."

The detective had accepted the gummas' explanation. Gumma Underwood gave back the CD. When Tou Vue met them walking out the door, the detective had his ears covered, and not because of the alarm bells. Both gummas were saying that they would sue him and the store and everybody else in St. Paul. The poor guy probably regretted he ever nabbed those two crazy ladies.

"What else could possibly go wrong?" Gumma Jackson said. "I'm taking all of you home and then

I'm going to *my* home to have a long hot bath."

"Can't get me out of here one minute too soon," Gumma Underwood said.

"What did you say?" Gumma Jackson asked her.

"I didn't say a word to you," Gumma Underwood answered.

"Better not ever again in life." Gumma Jackson arranged her scarves and stuck her nose up in the air. "Come on, Lawrence. Come on, Tou Vue. If that's in fact your name. This has been the worst birthday of my entire life!"

"And just whose fault is that?" asked Gumma Underwood.

"Well, let's just see. Could it possibly be a certain person who walked out of the store with a purse full of stolen merchandise? Hmmm."

"You got your nerve, Cordelia Jackson. It was one item and you know it. And I would have paid for it if you hadn't gotten me all flustered and made me forget."

"So your thieving ways are my fault, huh?" asked Gumma Jackson.

"What makes you think I won't slap you, Cordelia?" asked the other gumma.

It was so embarrassing. This was all taking place right in front of the entrance of the store. Most people were trying to be polite. They were trying to walk by and pretend they didn't see two old ladies yelling at each other. Other people were ruder. Some of them stood right there and watched. You could tell by the looks on their faces who they were rooting for.

"Stop it!" I yelled. The spectators looked at me now. "Can we just go home? NOW!"

Both gummas stopped yelling at each other and gave me a dirty look. Gumma Jackson took my hand and Gumma Underwood took Tou Vue's. They walked us to the car. Gumma Jackson burned rubber backing out of her parking space and burned some more pulling out of the lot. Gumma Underwood held on to her wig with every jerky car movement. No one said anything for a few minutes.

"Lawrence," Gumma Jackson said, "yelling at your gummas in public is unacceptable behavior."

"And so is lying," said Gumma Underwood.

"Your parents will be hearing about this, of course." Gumma Jackson looked at me in her rearview mirror.

I hoped she did tell them. I would tell them how terrible it was to spend the day with their crazy old mamas. I think Moms and Pops thought that since I'm a kid and because both gummas love me, that I could make us all get along okay. Well, I can't. It's not my stupid job.

"I don't care what you do," I told them. I tried to hold back the tears in front of Tou Vue. "And you can keep your stupid presents." I threw my binoculars and my radio in the front seat with them.

Tou Vue made his eyes real big. I felt bad for him

too. No one wants to watch someone else's family not get along.

"Now you've upset the child," Gumma Jackson said.

"Me? Why I've done no such thing. It's you doing the carrying on."

"Typical," Gumma Jackson mumbled. "Just typical."

"I suggest you remember who you're talking to," Gumma Underwood mumbled back.

"Believe me. I *know* who I'm dealing with. Ever since my daughter had the bad judgment to get mixed up with your people, my life has been one nightmare after the other."

"Oh, you want to talk about nightmares, do you? Well, my nightmare started right there at the wedding. And I remember I had called you up, Cordelia Jackson, and I had asked you directly what color flowers you were having in that church because I wanted to buy me a dress that matched. And you told me specifically that the color theme of the wedding was going to be pink and white. So I ordered me a pink dress. And then all the flowers turned out to be red and purple. I looked like a fool." Gumma Underwood started sobbing.

"Loretha, I sent you a message about that," said Gumma Jackson.

"No, you didn't," said Gumma Underwood.

"Yes, I did. I called and called you, and I didn't

get an answer. So I told Lorraine to tell you, and I told Wilton to tell you too. I reminded them twice as a matter of fact."

"Well, I never got that message," said Gumma Underwood.

"I'm sorry, Loretha. I meant to call you again, but I got so busy with last-minute plans. I didn't even know that your dress bothered you," said Gumma Jackson.

"Well. It did. And I never got any message."

"I am truly sorry. Your dress looked fine with the flowers and everything. When I saw it, I wished I'd had one just like it."

"You're just saying that," pouted Gumma Underwood.

"It's true. And even so, that little incident is nothing compared to what happened to me. You want to talk about nightmares. What about the day *my* grandson was born?" asked Gumma Jackson.

"You weren't even there."

"And just whose fault was that? As I remember, I called you and asked where *my* daughter and *my* grandbaby were. You sent me to the wrong hospital."

"I did not. I told you they were at the Children's Hospital, and that's where they were."

"In Minneapolis."

"So?"

"Loretha! There are *two* Children's Hospitals."

"There are?"

"You've been living in this area a hundred years and you mean to tell me you don't know there is a Children's Hospital in St. Paul?" asked Gumma Jackson.

"Cordelia! I live in Minneapolis. I don't drive a car. Only time I go to St. Paul is when my son takes me," said Gumma Underwood.

"I sat down in that hospital like a fool waiting all afternoon for my children. I thought something had happened to them." Gumma Jackson pulled the car off the road and reached in her purse for a tissue. She was making sniffing noises.

"Cordelia, I am so sorry. I wondered where you were that day. I thought you must really hate us an awful lot to not come see your own flesh and blood."

"I was down in that hospital all alone. I was so upset I didn't even remember there was another Children's. Finally a nurse reminded me. I was so mad. I thought you did it on purpose."

"I didn't. I'm sorry that happened to you, Cordelia. I'm sorry you missed out on that," said Gumma Underwood.

Both gummas dabbed at their cheeks with handkerchiefs. Gumma Jackson's wipes were more delicate. Still, you could see the black smudges where her makeup had smeared.

We parked there on the street for a long time. No one said anything. The gummas looked out the windows of the car.

I didn't know what they were thinking, but I bet it was about all the time they had wasted being mad at each other about stuff that had never even happened. If they were like me, they were probably trying to figure out what else they were wrong about, or if they could find any other reasons to stay mad.

Finally, Gumma Jackson started the car and we headed on home.

Party Time!

"PARTY?" GUMMA JACKSON said. "Loretha, what do you know about some birthday party?"

Just when I thought I was home free, something else happened. We got home at 5:00. Tou Vue had stashed his sleeping bag at my house, so we hurried to my room to get his and mine. If we left right away, we would be there before the tacos even got made!

"It's Tony R's birthday," I told Gumma Jackson. "We're really late." We started out the door.

"Just a minute, young man. Loretha, have you met this Tony R?" asked Gumma Jackson.

"I can't say as I have. Sounds like a gang member to me," said Gumma Underwood.

It's not a gang. It's a club.

"I don't know about you, Loretha, but I certainly have my concerns with the way parents nowadays are bringing up our young people."

Gumma Underwood said, "Amen."

"Lorraine's father and I never allowed our children in the homes of other people unless we got to know the families first."

Eek! I didn't like the way this was going one bit.

"We're really really late," I said.

"Yeah, late," Tou Vue added.

89

I wished he'd keep his mouth closed, because his talking reminded them of the trouble I was in. Fortunately, or unfortunately, they stayed with the matter at hand.

"I don't think Wilton and Lorraine use very good judgment sometimes," Gumma Underwood said.

"Well, they're young," Gumma Jackson said. "They'll learn. In the meantime, let's you and me escort our young gentlemen friends here to this so-called party. We best check the circumstances ourselves, don't you think?"

"Oh no!" Tou Vue and I groaned. We collapsed on the floor on top of our sleeping bags. What kind of party could Tony R have with two old ladies there?

"I suggest a couple of young men I know watch their attitudes," Gumma Underwood said. "I think they've made quite enough mischief for one day."

What choice did we have? As much as we didn't want to, we showed the gummas the way to Tony R's house.

We rang the doorbell.

"It certainly looks pleasant enough," Gumma Jackson said.

"But, you know, you never can tell," responded Gumma Underwood. "Right next to me over in Minneapolis is a cute little bungalow just like this. Inside, it's nothing but heathens."

"Go on!" Gumma Jackson said.

"God's honest truth. I can't even go in my own

backyard sometimes in the summer."

What a dumb conversation. I almost liked it better when they hated each other. Almost.

"*Buenas tardes,*" Mr. Rodriguez said. That means "good afternoon." Mrs. Rodriguez said, "*Pásale,*" which means "come on in."

"They're Mexicans," said Gumma Underwood. I gave her a real dirty look. I think the Rodriguezes already knew they were Mexicans before she announced it to the whole world.

I could hear the rest of the Wildcats downstairs, already whooping it up. I heard Kevin's loud laugh. It sounds like the noise a horse makes. The house smelled great—like fried onions and corn tortillas.

Mr. Rodriguez offered the gummas seats on the living room couch. They pulled me down between them. I wanted to be where the fun was. I felt one gumma's hand on each shoulder, holding me down. Tou Vue kept right on going.

"See ya!" he said.

So much for old buddy, old pal. Friends were hard to come by in a fix like mine.

"We're Lawrence's grandmothers. We understand that you're having some of the neighborhood children over," spoke up Gumma Jackson.

"I am charmed, ladies." Mr. Rodriguez grabbed each gumma's hand in turn and clasped it between two of his. "Today, my son, Antonio, celebrates his twelfth birthday. We are having a big fiesta."

"*Café?*" Tony's mother offered. She set a tray with steaming cups in front of the gummas and went back to the kitchen.

"We like to know where our Larry is spending his time," Gumma Underwood said. "A person can't be too careful these days."

Tony R's dad made a clicking noise with his tongue. "Ladies, I am a police officer, and I couldn't agree with you more. Things are pretty rough out there. But today is a day for celebration. I insist you ladies join us for supper."

Both gummas shook their heads and said that was a mighty kind offer, and that they couldn't stay, but he was really thoughtful.

"He's a cute thing," Gumma Underwood whispered. Someone should have given her whispering lessons. They probably could have heard her down in the basement!

"I must insist," said Mr. Rodriguez. "My son's party would not be complete without the addition of such lovely *señoras* as yourselves."

Both gummas batted their eyes and acted all shy.

"You, young man," Mr. Rodriguez pulled me up from the couch, "are missing all the fun. You take that sleeping bag downstairs with the rest of the boys. I will entertain these two young ladies."

You'd better believe I followed his orders, and fast.

Downstairs were all the guys: Tony R, Johnny Vang, Bobby, Kevin, and, of course, Tou Vue, who had already gotten in a Gameboy match with Kevin.

"You're late!" Tony R said.

I told him I was sorry and that it was a long story. Tou Vue nodded. Maybe I'd tell it someday, but for now, it was time for the games to begin!

First we went out in the backyard and played soccer. It was me and Johnny Vang and Kevin against Tou Vue, Bobby, and the birthday boy. Some of the guys like soccer, but I'm only lukewarm about it. It's fun enough, but I prefer regular old football any day, where you can pick up the ball and run. The great thing about soccer is there is a lot of bumping into people and falling down. It gives you a good excuse to roll around on the ground and get dirty. Just the thing guys love.

Before we knew it, Mrs. Rodriguez was yelling that it was time for tacos. We all rushed for the table.

"All hands washed first," she said. She posted Gumma Jackson at the bathroom door to do the hand check. Gumma was tough. Even a little bit of a smear and you had to go back. It took Kevin three tries.

The tacos were fantastic! Mrs. Rodriguez makes real Mexican tacos, and they are nothing like the ones you get at a fast-food place. Hers are very spicy and full of flavor. Her tortillas are fresh and tender, and she knows to make plenty of food.

"Look at these *muchachos* eat!" Mr. Rodriguez said. He said it proudly, and we each ate another taco and guzzled more pop.

Later on, we listened to Tony R's aunts and uncles sing the birthday song, as usual. Even though it was sung in Spanish, I had heard it enough years that I knew the words.

Estás son las mañanitas
Que cantaba el Rey Davíd
Hoy, por ser día de tus santo
Te las cantamos a ti.

Then came the big surprise.

"Can I have everybody's attention!" Gumma Jackson announced.

Eek! I thought. What was this all about?

"Loretha and I didn't bring a gift, but we have a special present anyway, just for Antonio."

Gumma Underwood stood up. She started singing. "Do dum da do da do da, do dum da do da do da, dat da!"

And then she and Gumma Jackson sang this old song called "My Guy!"

Everybody clapped and sang along. All the adults seemed to know the words.

"No handsome face could ever take the place of my guy!"

The gummas danced around with their hands on their hips and their purses hanging off their arms. It was all off-key and everything, but it was great! I couldn't stop smiling!

At the end, they whisper-sang, "There's not a man today who can tear me away from my guy."

"What you say?" everybody yelled, and they whisper-sang it again.

It might have been a song for Tony R, but I couldn't help thinking a little bit of it was for me too.

The Last Part

THAT'S ALMOST EVERYTHING I have to tell. The party was slamming as always, and with all the usual stuff too. Around midnight we snuck out of the basement and over to Jenny Pederson's backyard. We had found Tony R's old Halloween mask of a dead zombie guy covered with green pus and slime. Bobby got boosted up to Jenny's window. We put the flashlight in his face and knocked on her window. She was ready for us, as usual. She opened her window and blasted us with about a dozen water balloons, but we blasted her right back with the Super Soaker. She screamed and her dad turned on the back porch light.

"I'll get you guys," she threatened.

We scurried back to Tony R's, wet and laughing. There was no end to the fun.

Every year I wonder where Kevin gets his gifts. This year he found cans of green-and-yellow-colored goop that looked like snot! We had it dripping out of our noses and ears and everywhere. And when we threw it on the wall, it just stuck there. It was great. I wanted some of it in every color.

Tony R liked it too, but he told me and Tou Vue that the Super Soaker was his favorite gift of all.

Gumma had supper ready when I got home the next night. I tried to eat some, but I was full. As always, we'd ended the day at the Mall of America. We went to a movie, and Tony R's dad bought us giant tubs of popcorn and large pops. We had already eaten pizza and donuts and all kinds of other junk. Johnny Vang threw up in the bathroom at the mall, but I'm not supposed to tell anybody that.

While I picked at my supper, Gumma took all the dishes out of the kitchen cupboards.

"What are you doing?" I asked her.

"Rearranging Lorraine's things so they'll be easier for her to find."

I just shook my head. I hoped I'd be someplace else when Moms found out.

Moms and Pops pulled in from Milwaukee right on schedule—7:30, like they said. Gumma Jackson had driven back to our house in time to greet them.

I stood in the front yard, between the gummas. Each one had an arm around me.

"I want you to listen to me, Lawrence," Gumma Jackson said. "You let *me* do all the talking. I don't want you to say one word about what happened yesterday. Understand?"

"Uh-huh," I said.

"You do what your gumma tells you, you hear?" Gumma Underwood said. Both their smiles looked sort of phony, if you asked me.

Moms and Pops got out of the car. They both looked kinda pulled apart, the way people do when they've been on a long car ride. Pops looked at Moms and then looked back at us. He squinted. We were all three smiling big smiles. I guess we looked suspicious.

"You all seem happy," Pops said. "Which of you wants to . . ."

But before he could say anything else, the gummas were all over them.

"Wilton!"

"Lorraine!"

They hugged their children and slobbered them with some of those juicy kisses. Pops gave me a questioning look, but I just shrugged.

Later, at bedtime, I plugged in my new clock radio. Yes, the gummas did give me my gifts back. Of course they did. I told them they did not have to compete over me, and they didn't have to buy my love. They said they knew that and what a precious boy I was and how I was the light of their lives.

They never said a word to Moms and Pops about the lie I told about Tou Vue. It's our little secret.

So what's a guy to do? Maybe I *am* a little spoiled, but if the choice was not having the gummas at all or being spoiled by them, I'd pick being spoiled any day.

The digital lights of the clock radio made my room glow red in the dark. At first it was spooky, but I got used to it. On Sunday nights some of the stations play oldies. I turned on the radio and set it so that it would turn off by itself in an hour. I think I heard the song the gummas sang at Tony R's party, but I'm not too sure. It had been a busy weekend, and I was tired, so I could have just remembered it in my head.